Does a Sea Cow Say MOO?

Terry Webb Harshman

illustrated by George McClements

BLOOMSBURY
CHILDREN'S
BOOKS

To my Father, who showed his little girl the sea,
and to my brother Mick, who shared its wonders with me
—T. W. H.

For my beautiful mermaid, Rachel, and my guppies, Samuel and Matthew
—G. M.

Published by Bloomsbury U.S.A. Children's Books
175 Fifth Avenue, New York, New York 10010
Distributed to the trade by Macmillan

Library of Congress Cataloging-in-Publication Data
Harshman, Terry Webb.
Does a sea cow say moo? / by Terry Webb Harshman ;
illustrated by George McClements. — 1st U.S. ed.
p.   cm.
Summary: When Flash arrives on the beach by spaceship, he quizzes Jack about why some
names on the sea are the same as on land, such as a school of fish and a school in town,
or a cow in the sea and a cow in a field. Includes "wacky fish facts."
ISBN-13: 978-1-58234-740-0 • ISBN-10: 1-58234-740-9 (hardcover)
ISBN-13: 978-1-59990-278-4 • ISBN-10: 1-59990-278-8 (reinforced)
[1. Homonyms—Fiction. 2. Marine animals—Fiction. 3. Extraterrestrial beings—Fiction.
4. Stories in rhyme.] I. McClements, George, ill. II. Title.
PZ8.3.H248Doe 2008   [E]—dc22   2007040269

Typeset in Birdlegs
Art created with mixed media
Book design by Nicole Gastonguay

First U.S. Edition 2008
Printed in China
1 3 5 7 9 10 8 6 4 2   (hardcover)
1 3 5 7 9 10 8 6 4 2   (reinforced)

All papers used by Bloomsbury U.S.A. are natural, recyclable products
made from wood grown in well-managed forests. The manufacturing processes
conform to the environmental regulations of the country of origin.

A spaceship touched down
On the beach with a *splash!*
The pilot saw Jack
And said, “My name’s Flash!

I’ve come to find out
Why some names in the sea
Are the same as on land . . .
Will you please help me?”

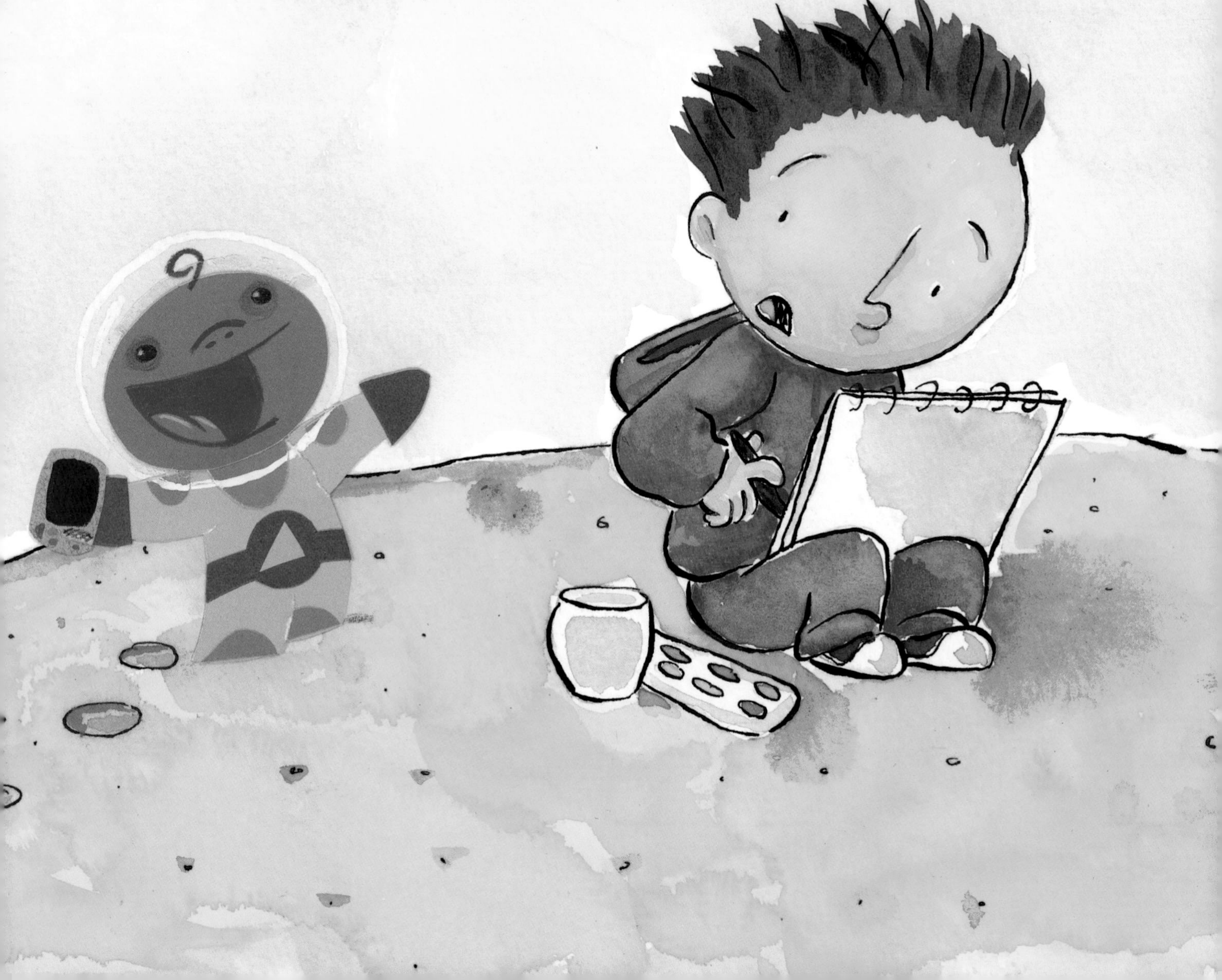

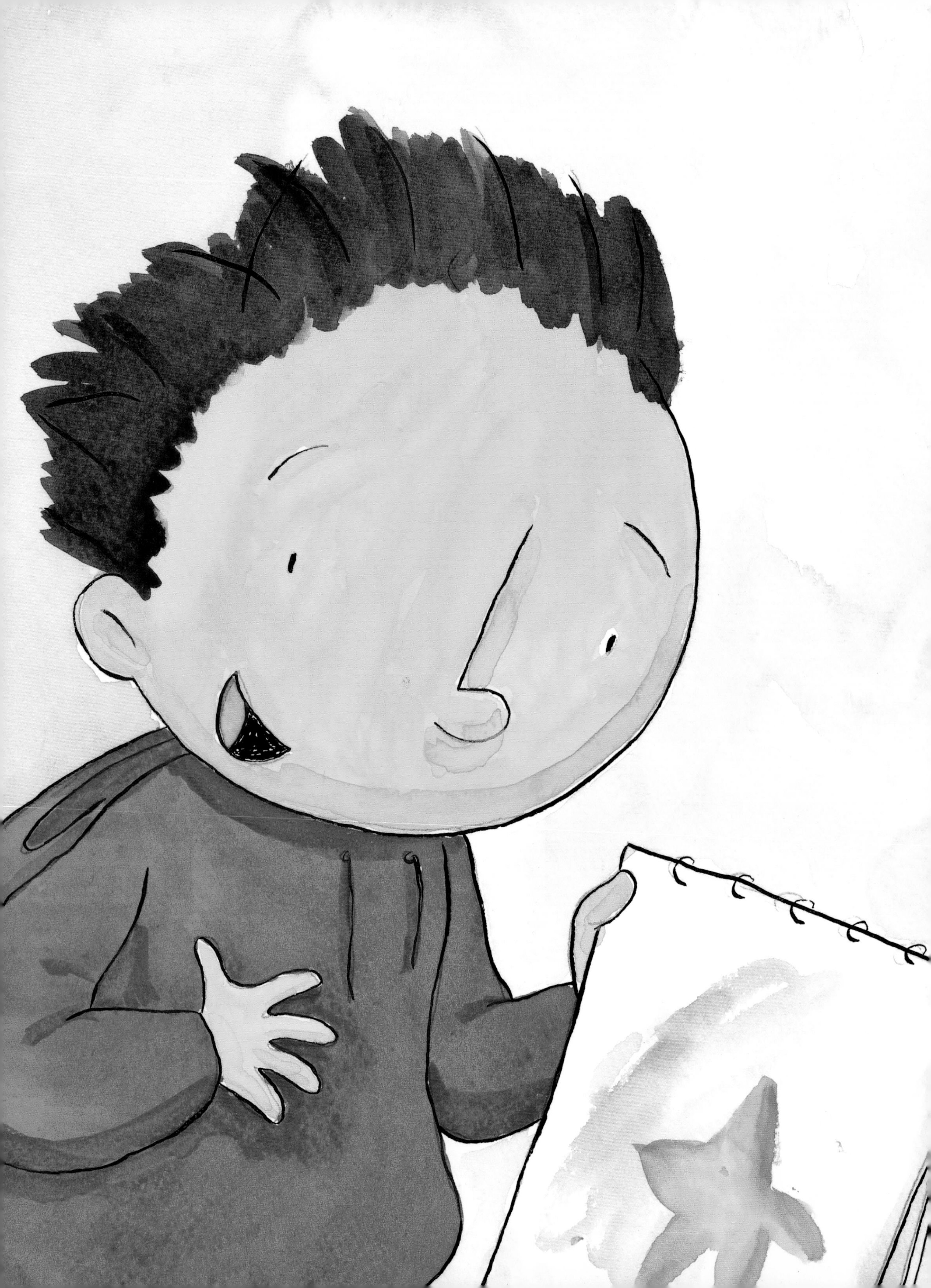

"You need help, you say?
Then it's your lucky day!

My friends call me Jack,
And I'll be your guide
To some of the creatures
Who live in the tide!"

“SCHOOL in the sea.
SCHOOL in your town.
Does a school of fish study
In classrooms deep down?”

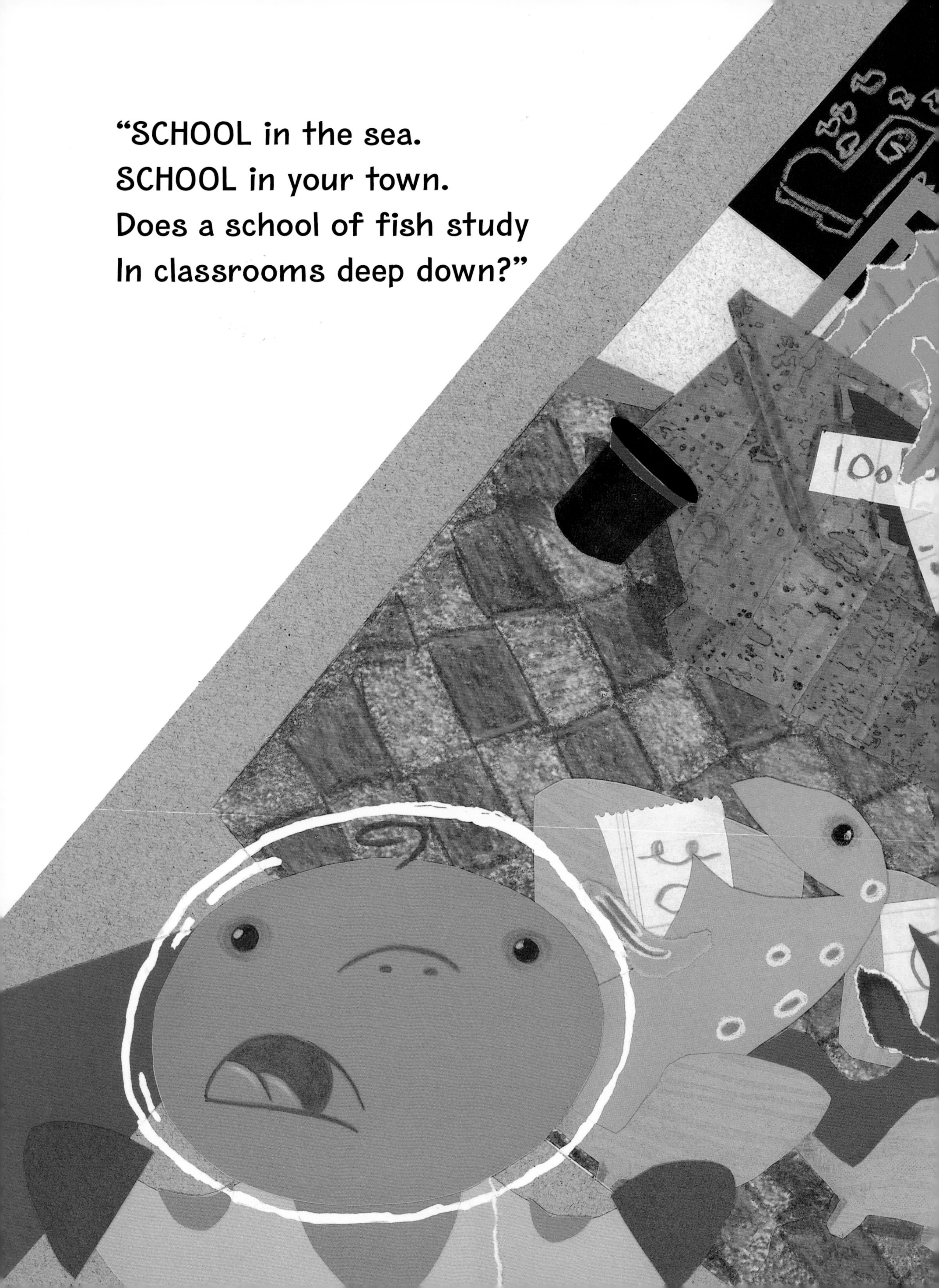

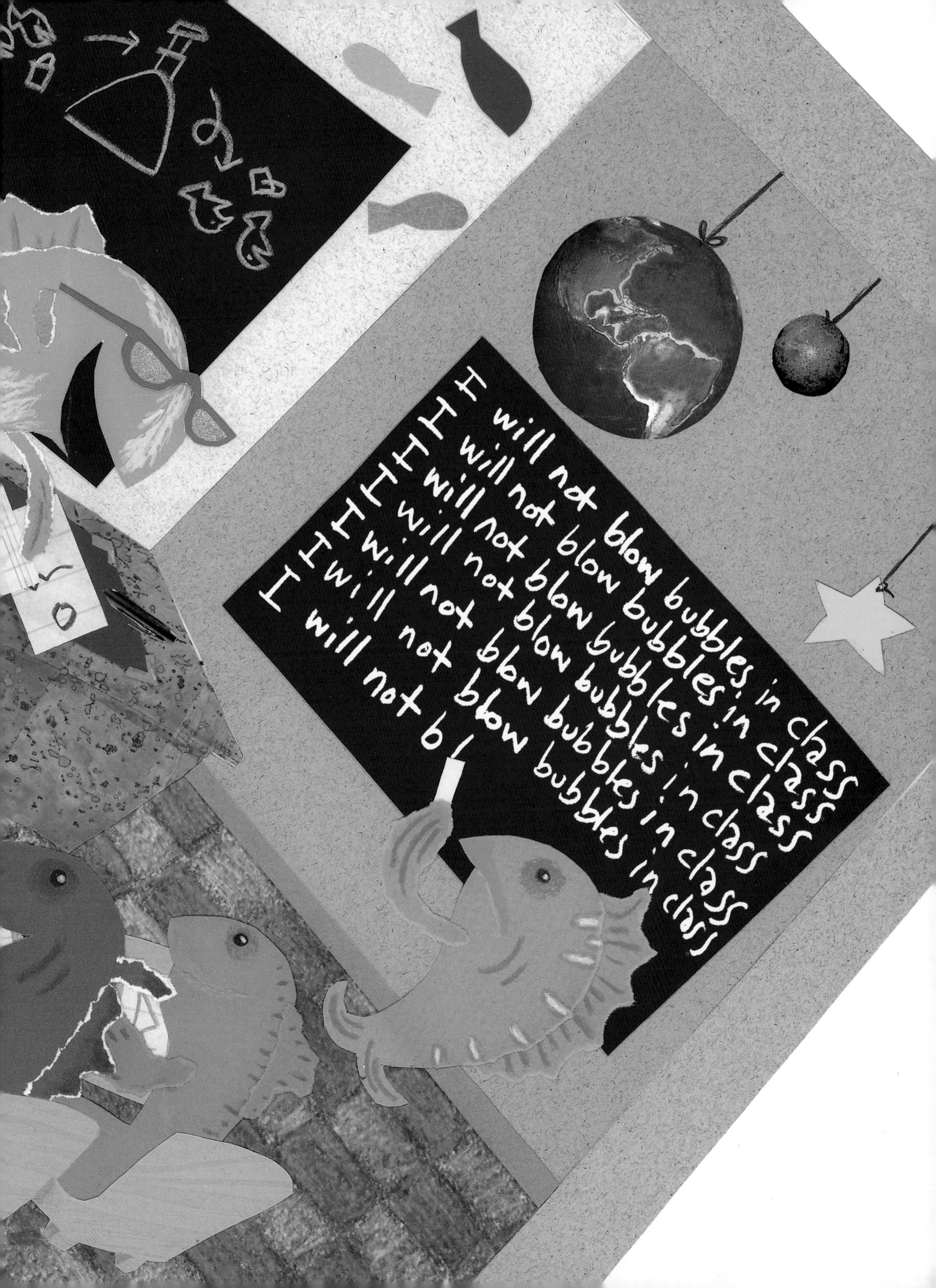

I will not blow bubbles in class
I will not blow bubbles in class
I will not blow bubbles in class
I will not blow bubbles in class
I will not blow bubbles in class
I will not blow bubbles in class
I will not b

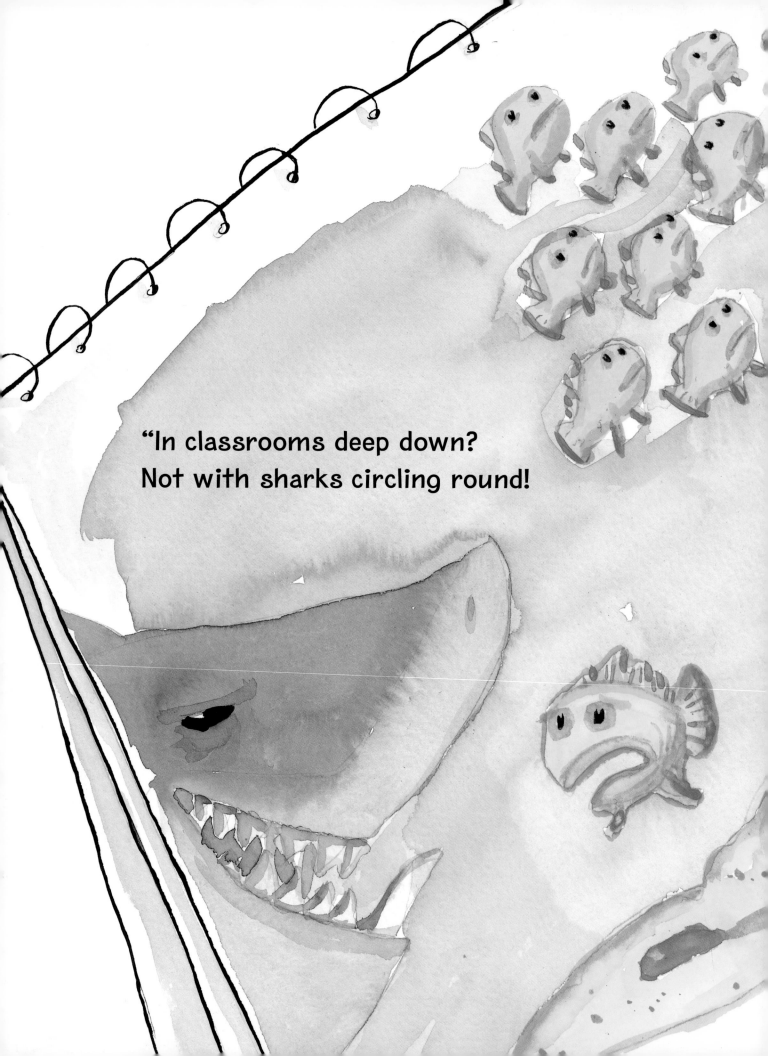

"In classrooms deep down?
Not with sharks circling round!

A school is when fishes
Go swimming in bunches;
Fish swimming solo
Can end up as lunches!"

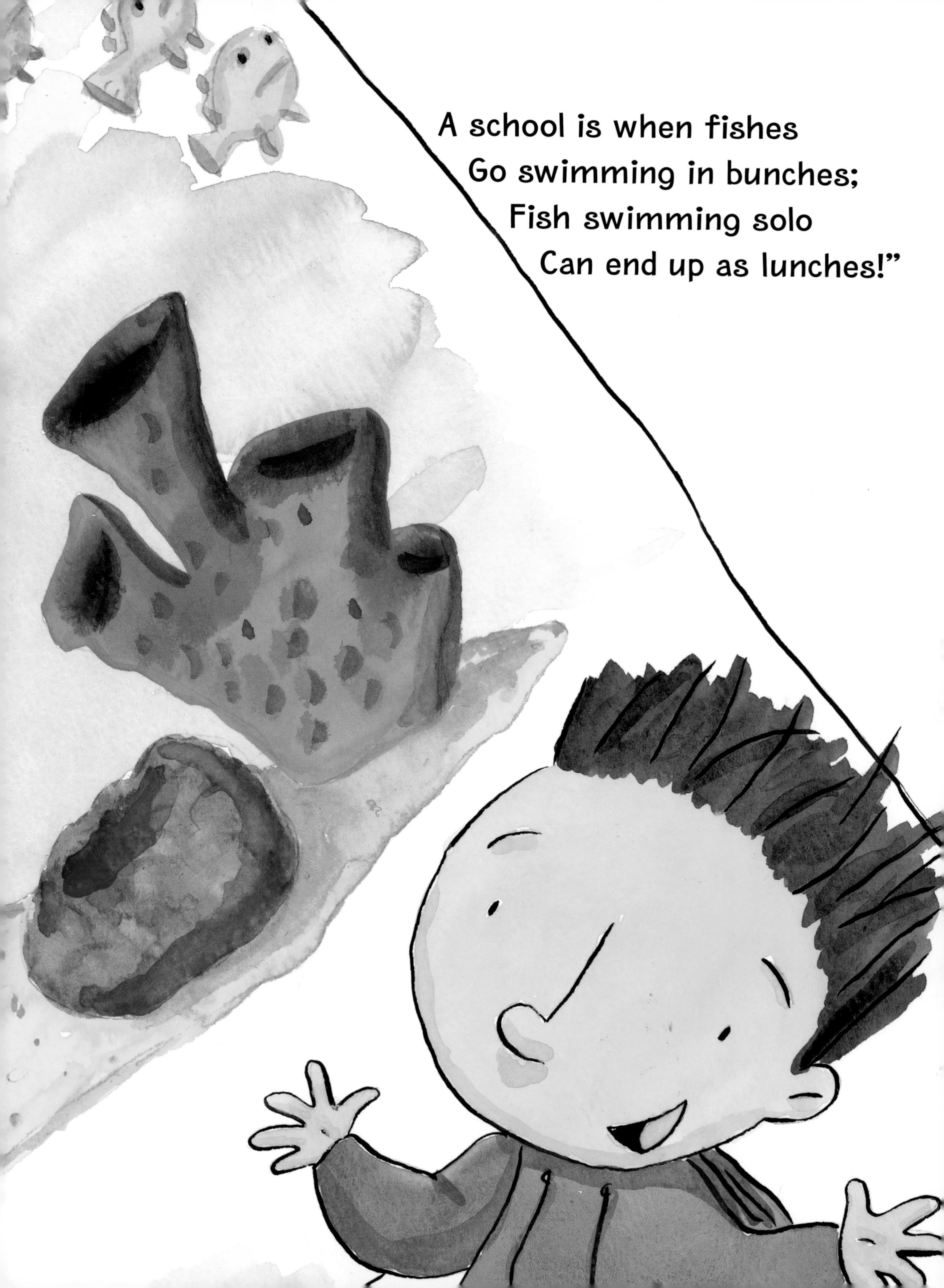

"COW in the sea.
COW in the field.
Does a sea cow say *moo*
And eat grass for its meal?"

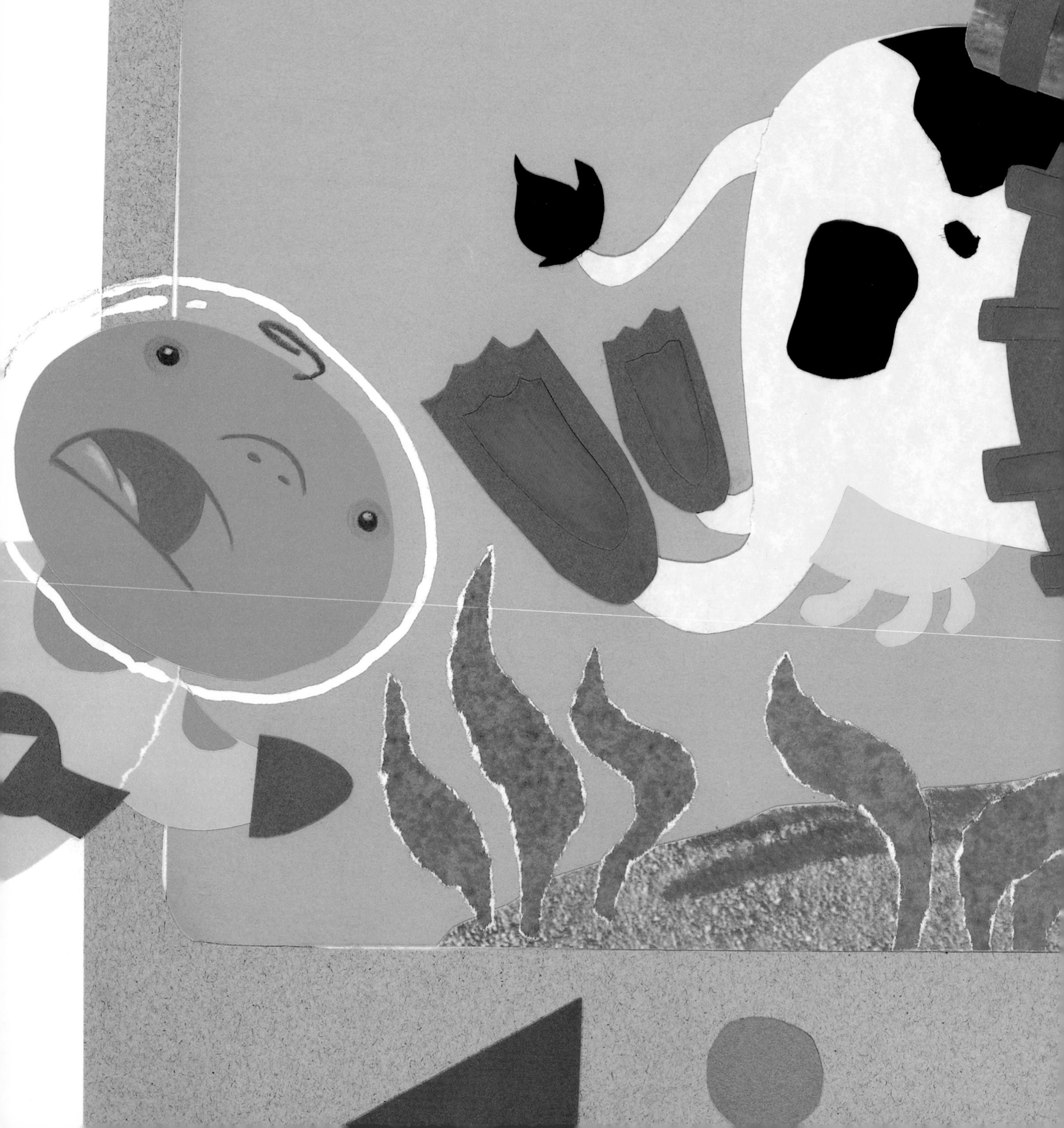

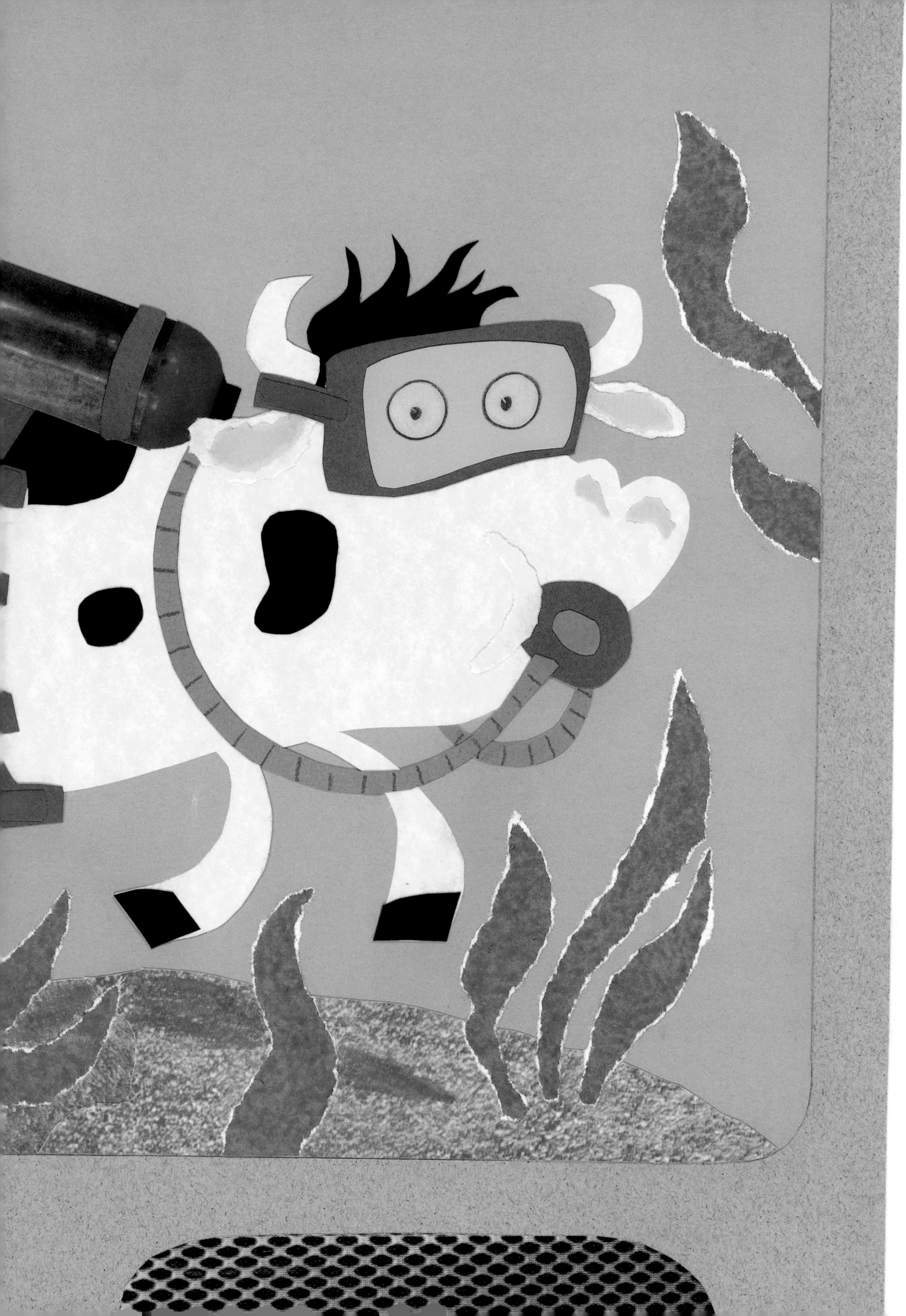

"A sea cow say *moo*?
No, that isn't true!

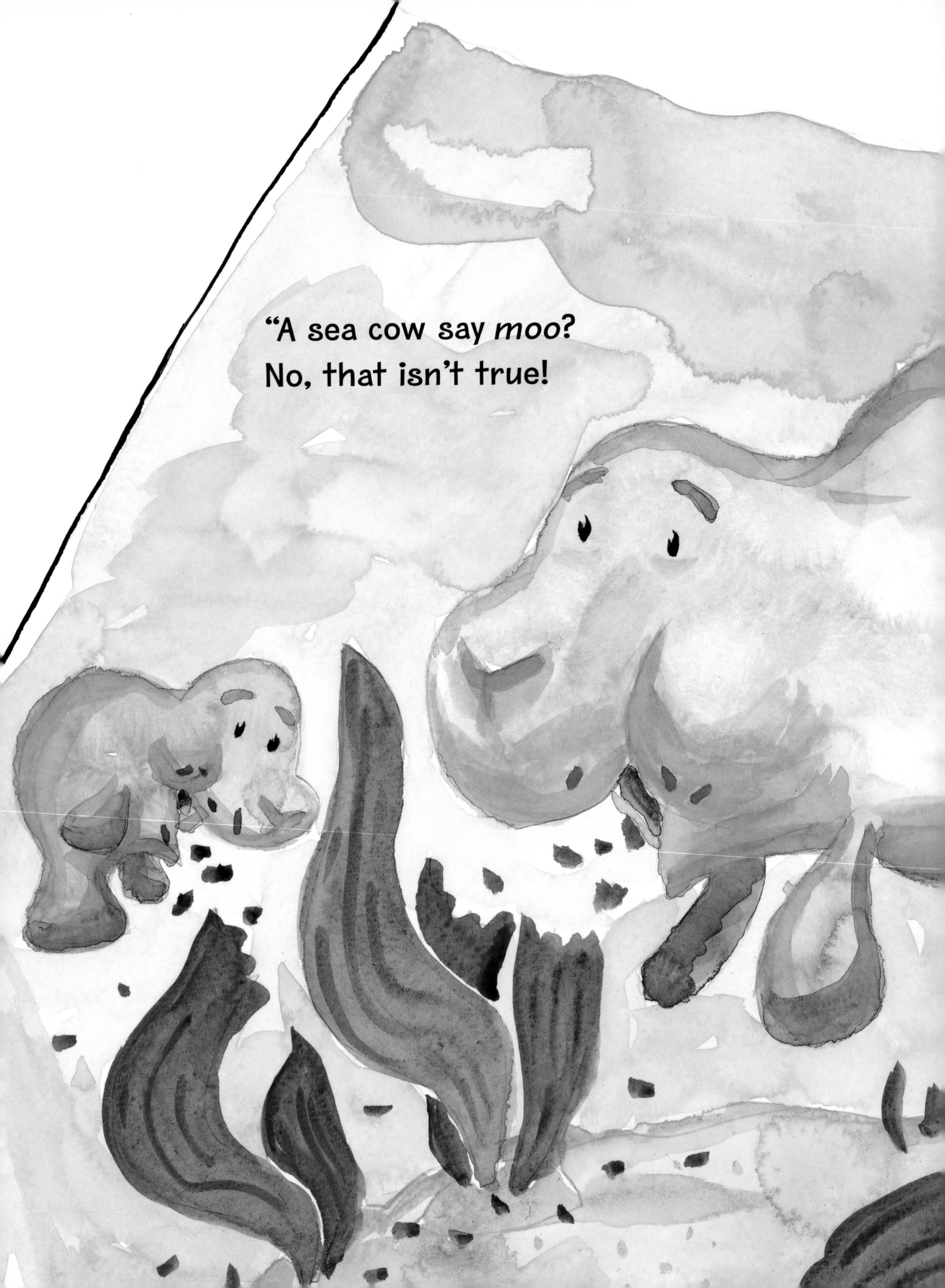

It chirps and it clicks
And it whistles instead
And grazes on sea plants
In shallow sea beds."

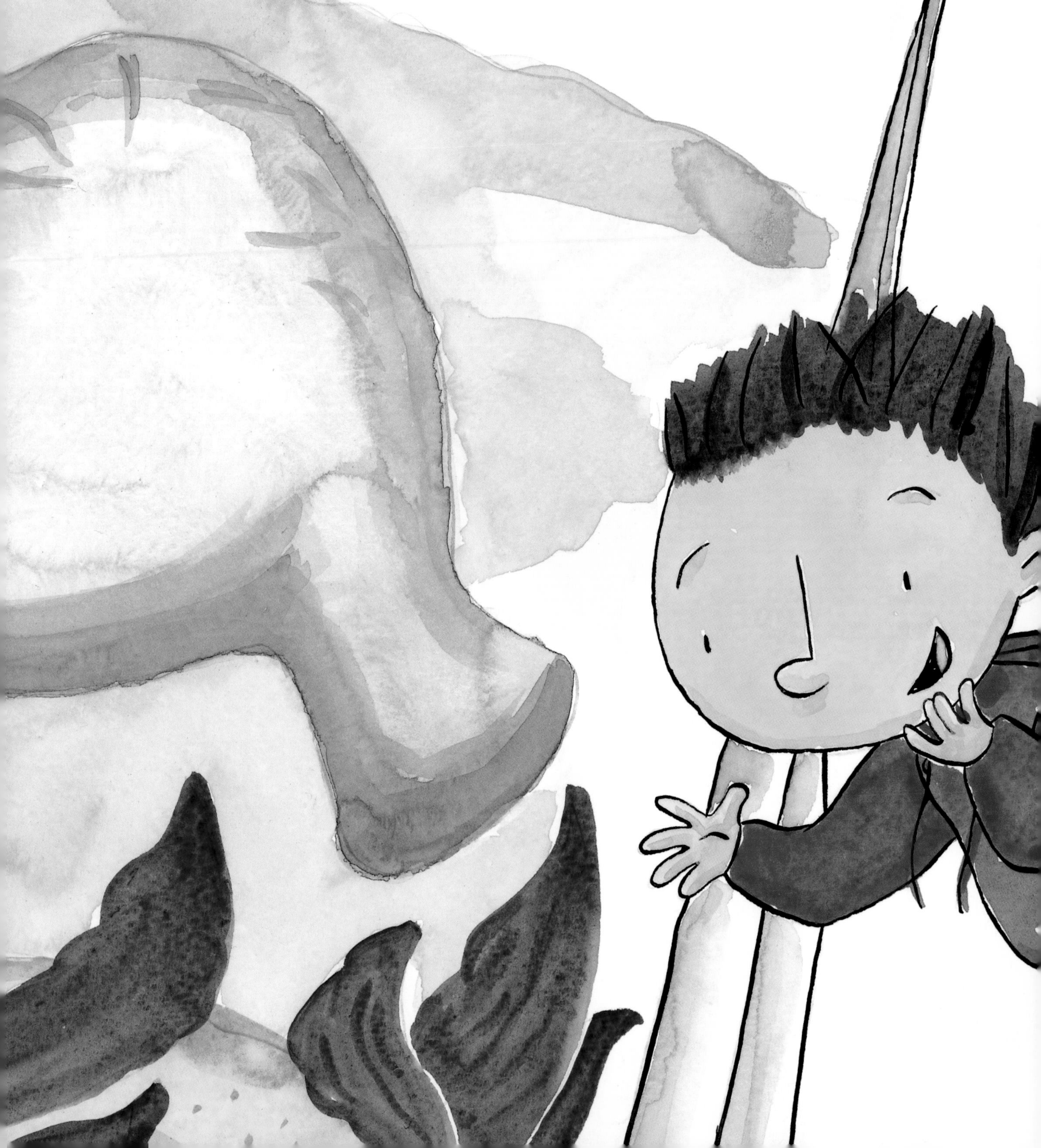

"CLOWN in the sea.
CLOWN at the fair.
Do clown fish wear bow ties
And curly red hair?"

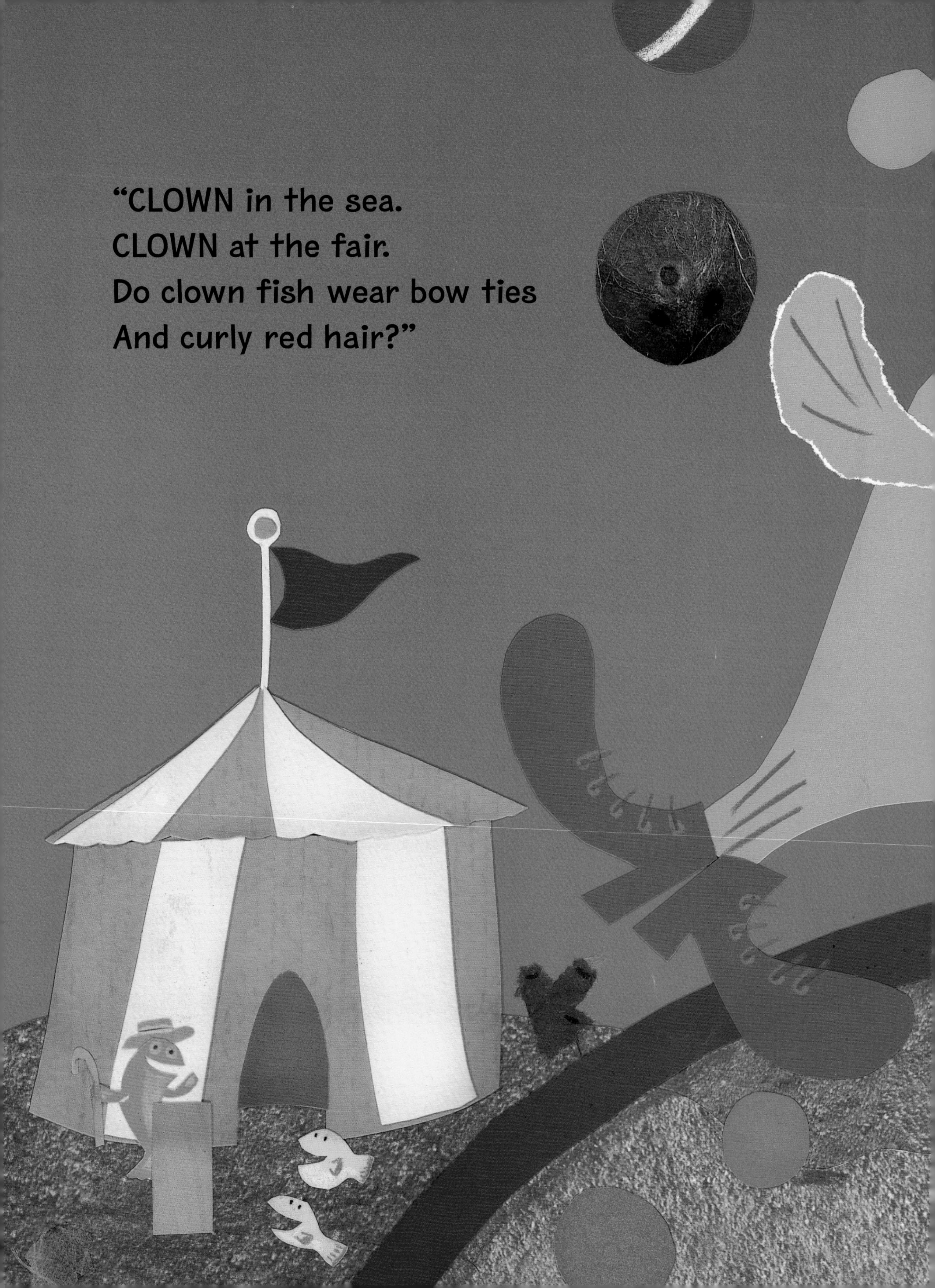

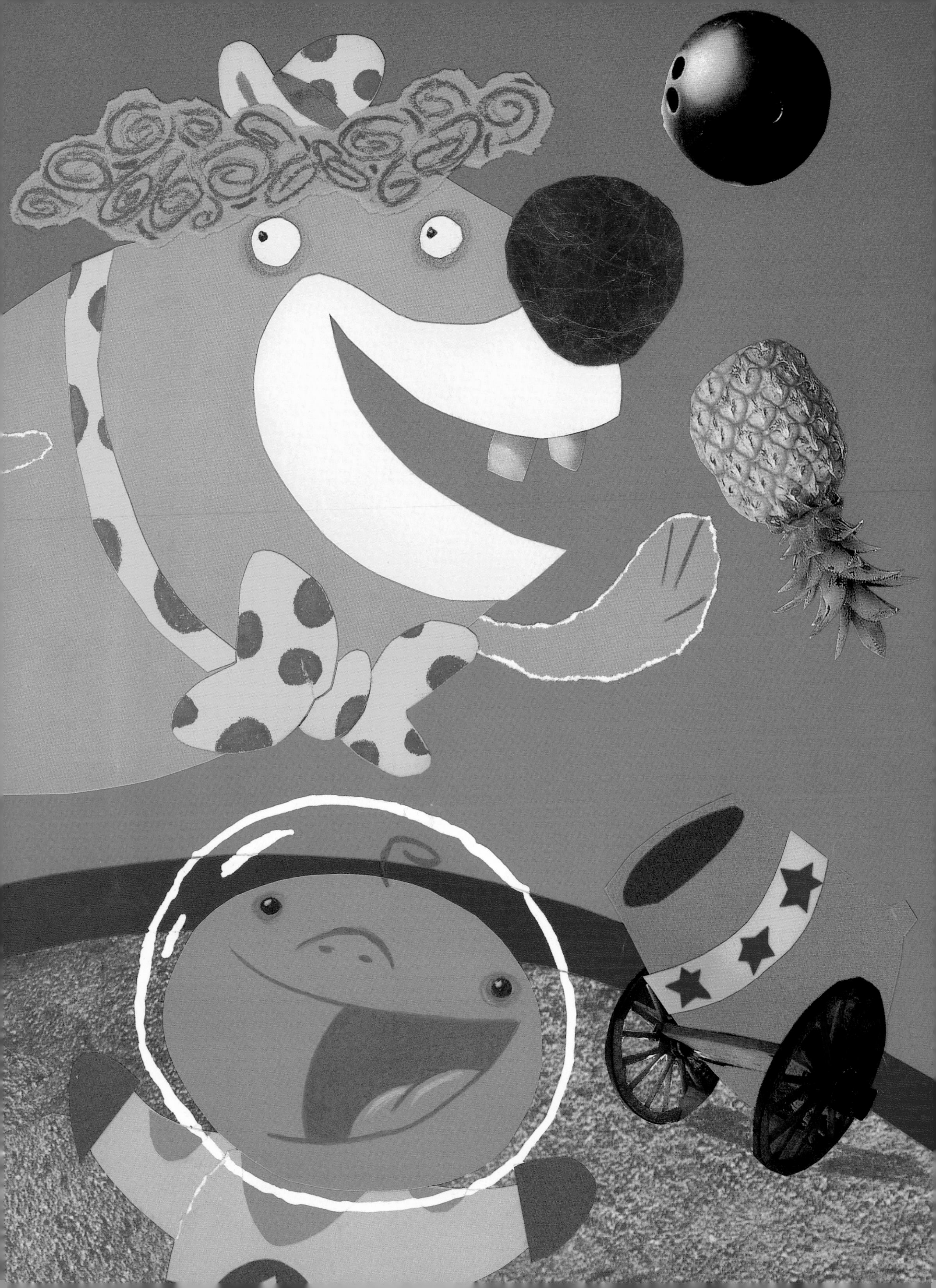

"Wear bow ties and hair?
This fish wouldn't dare!

Predators spot his
Bright colors with ease!
For protection he darts
In a-nem-o-nes."

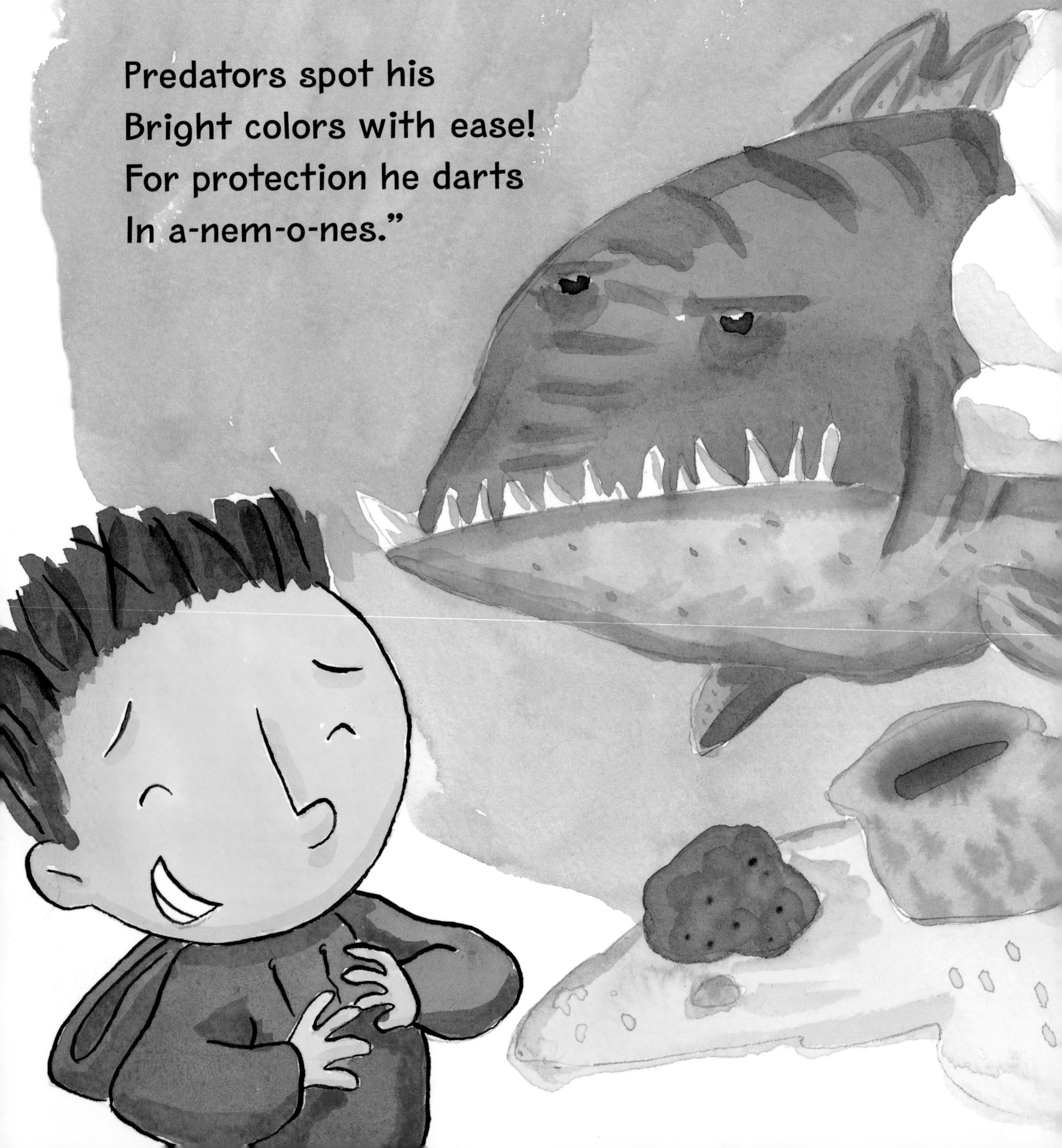

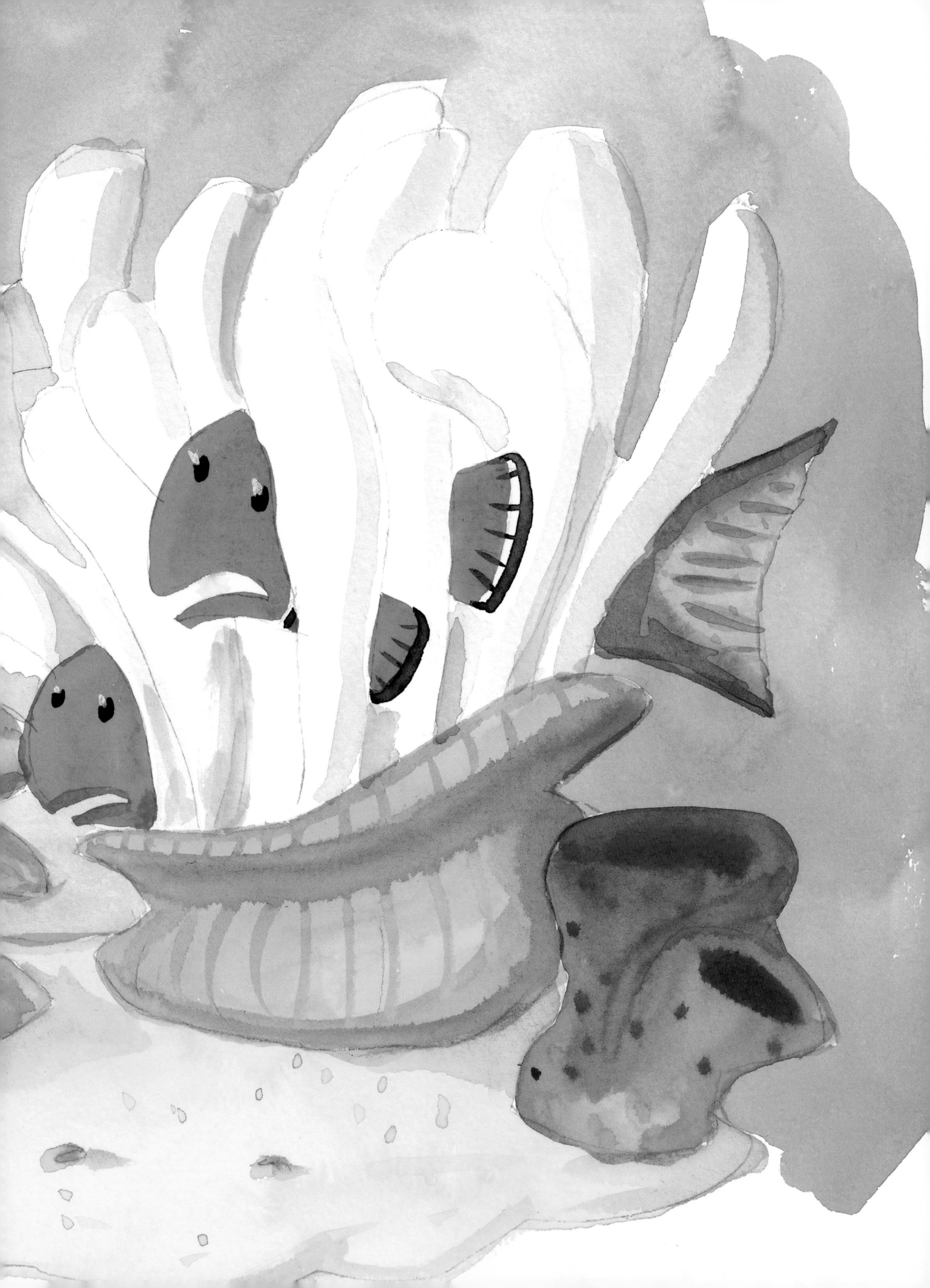

"HORSE in the sea.
HORSE in the hay.
Can you saddle a sea horse
And gallop away?"

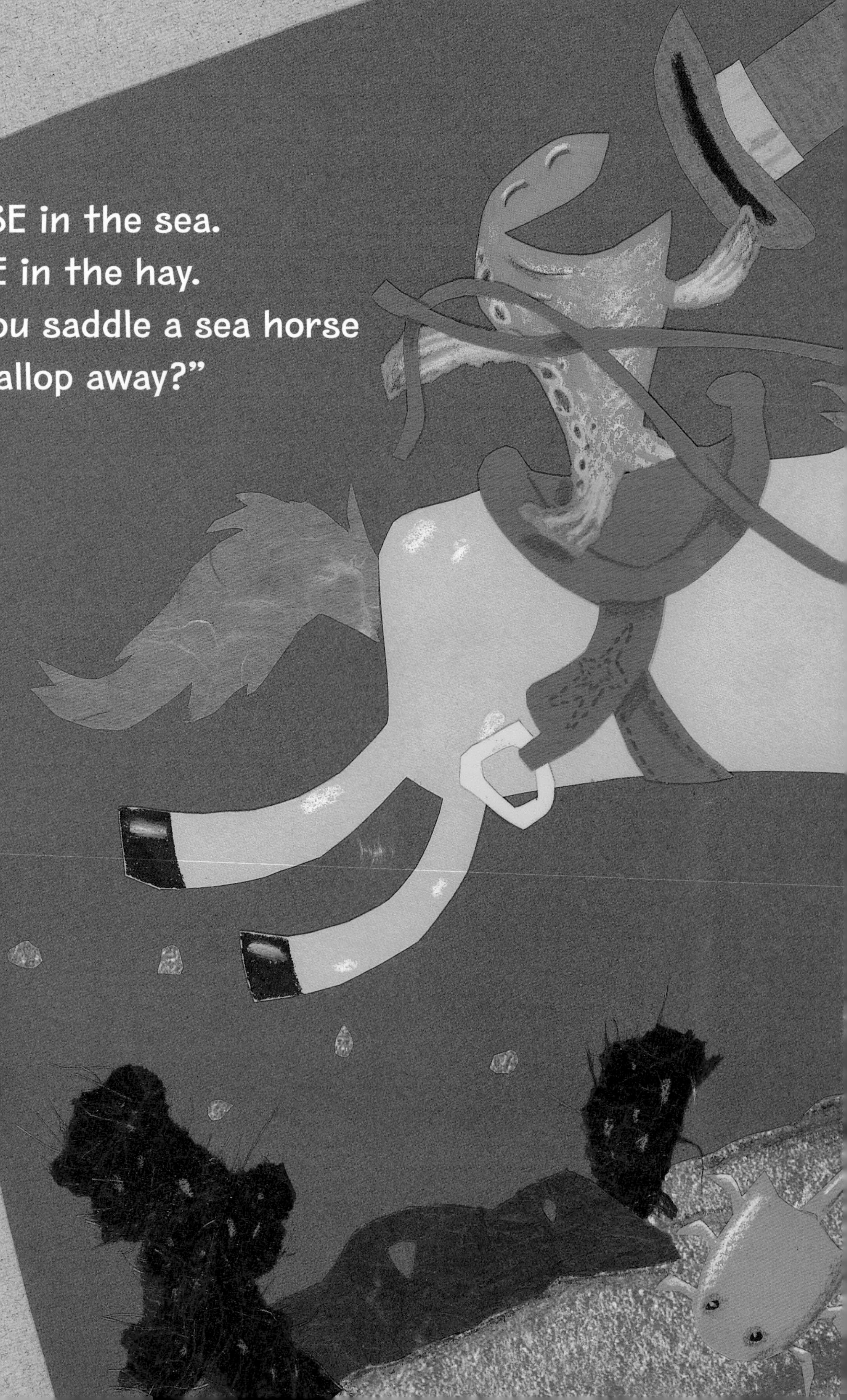

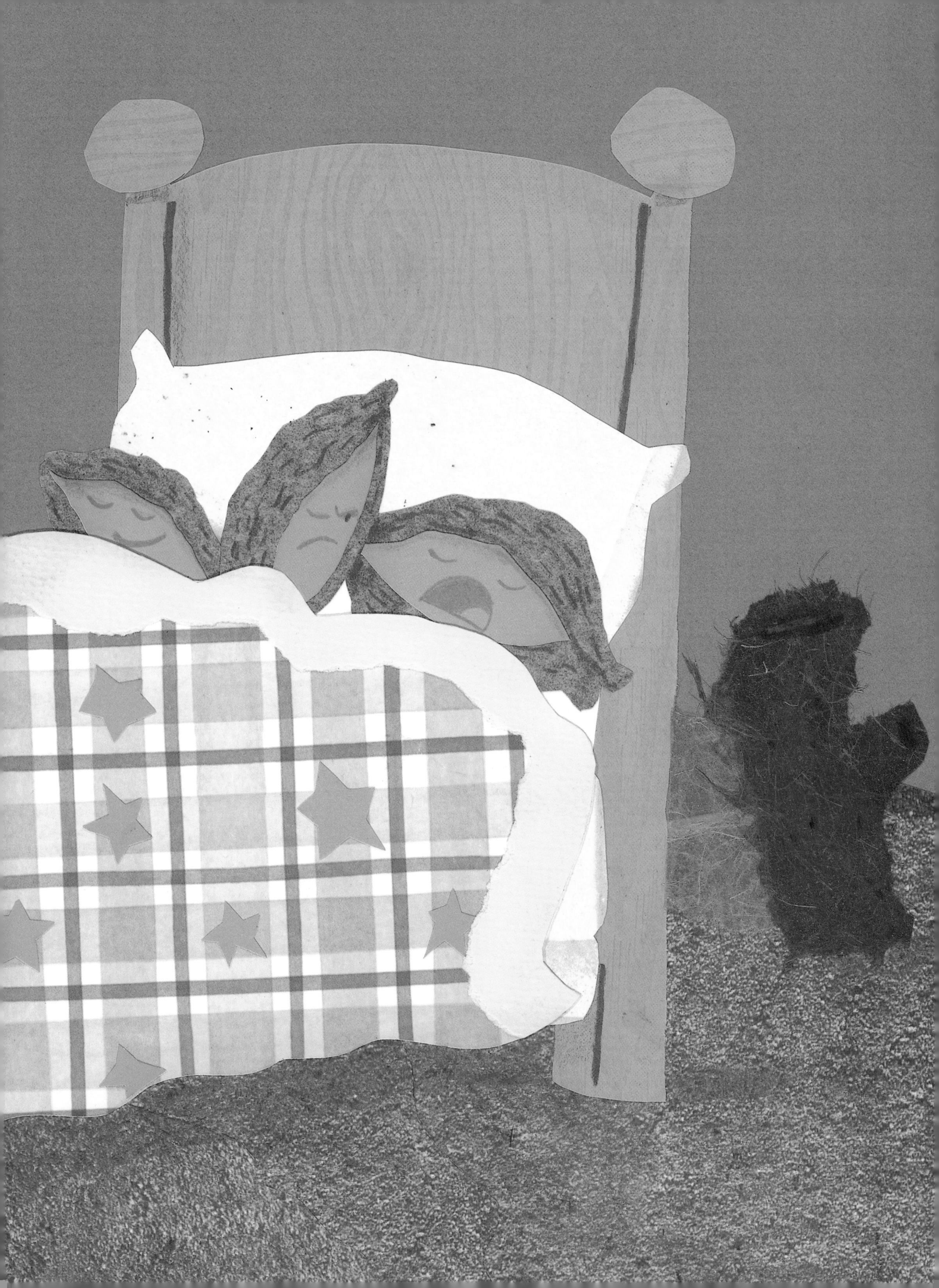

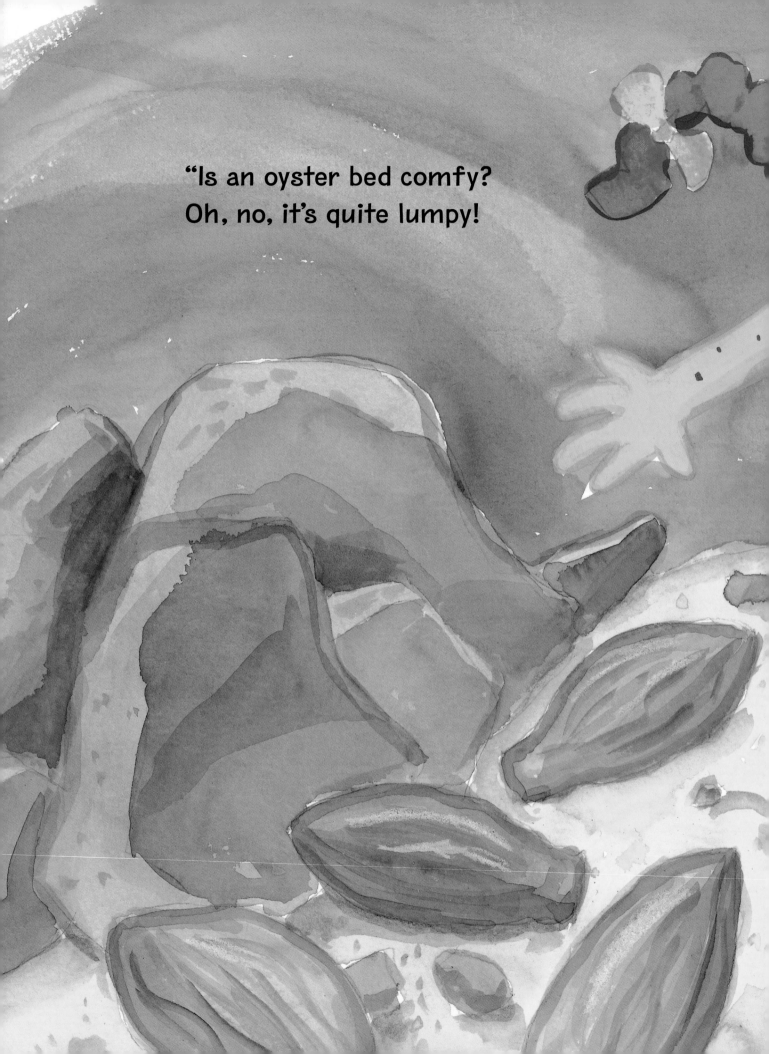

"Is an oyster bed comfy?
Oh, no, it's quite lumpy!

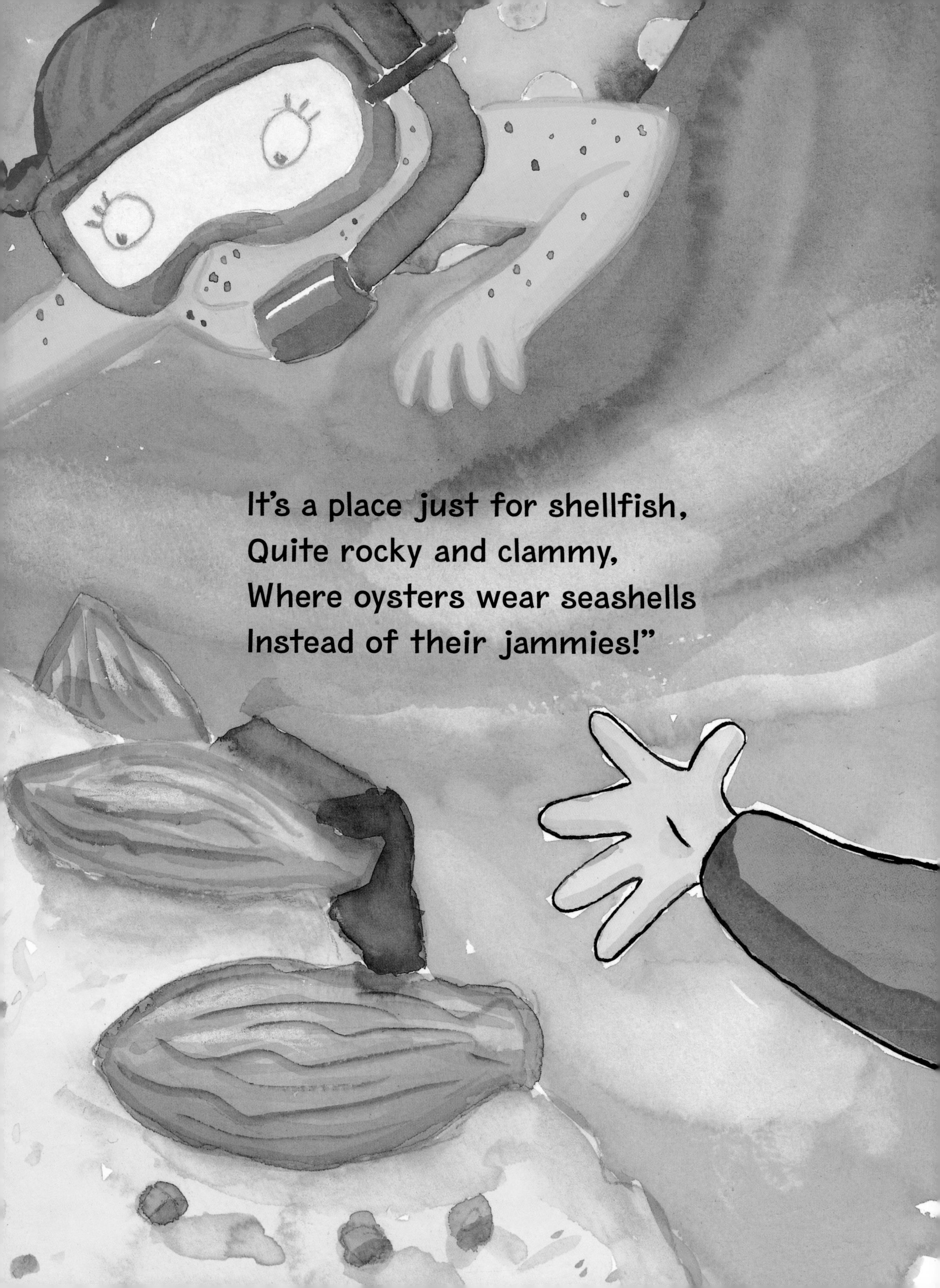

It's a place just for shellfish,
Quite rocky and clammy,
Where oysters wear seashells
Instead of their jammies!"

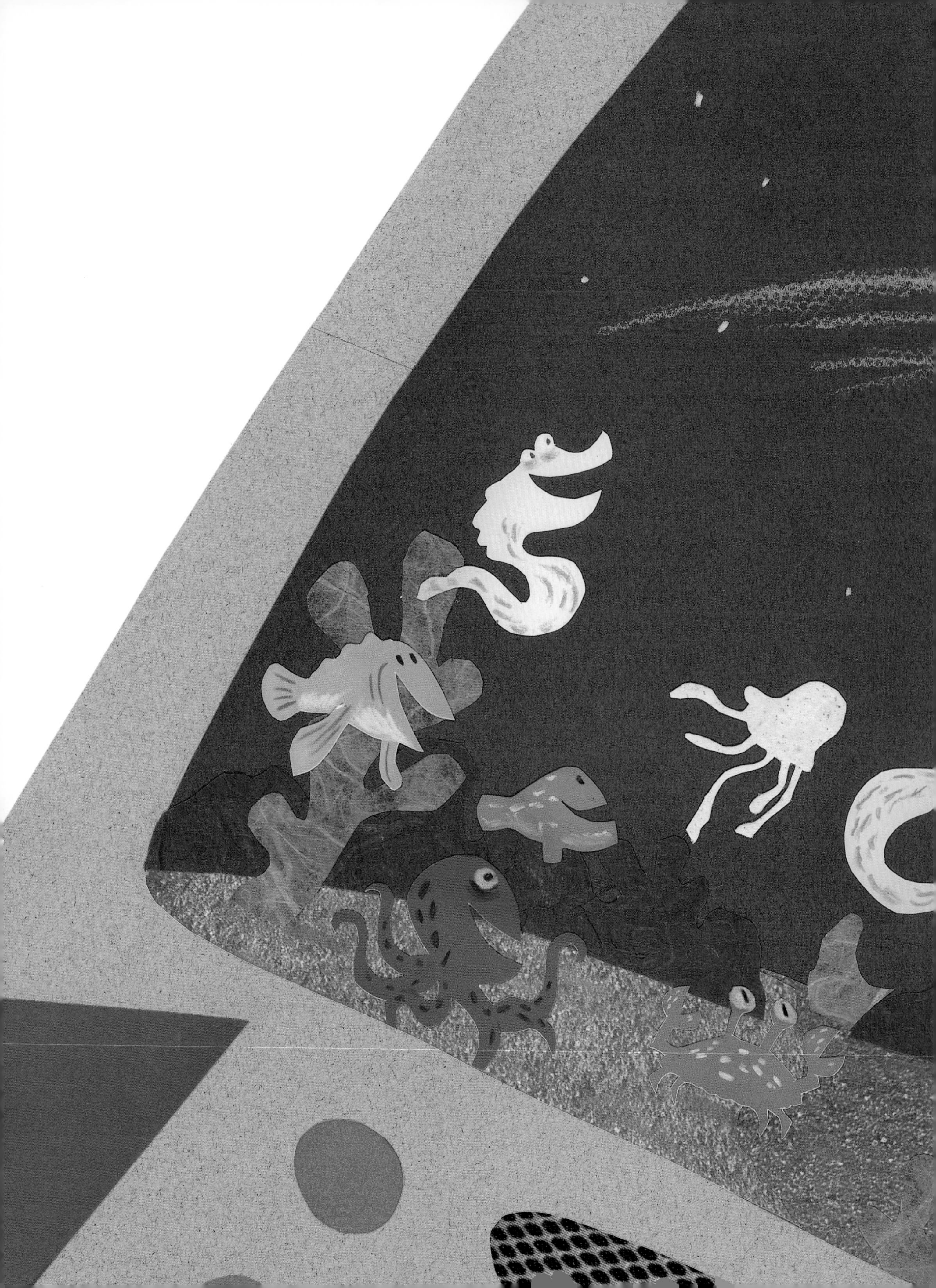

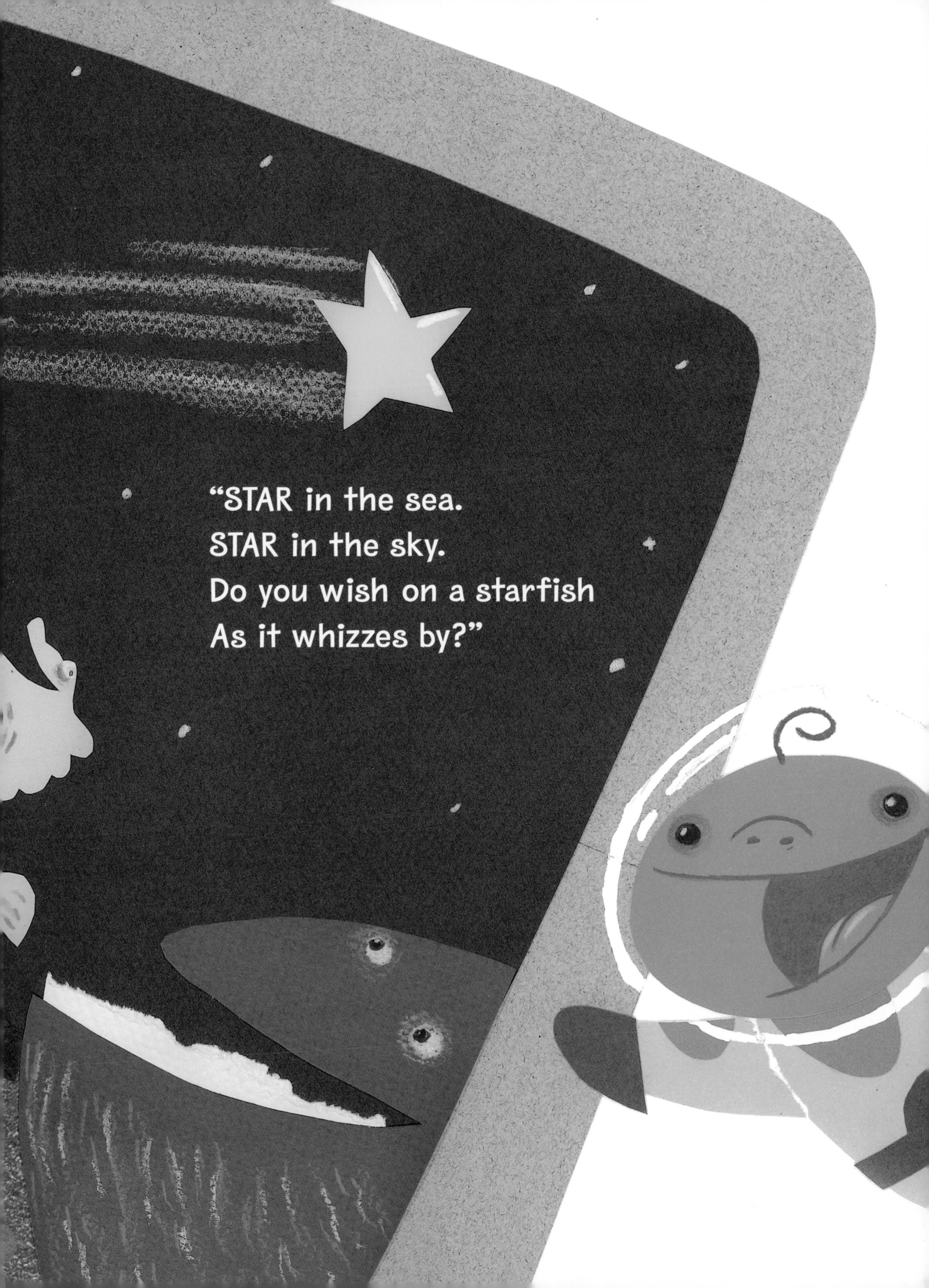

"STAR in the sea.
STAR in the sky.
Do you wish on a starfish
As it whizzes by?"

"As it whizzes by?
This star's slow and shy!

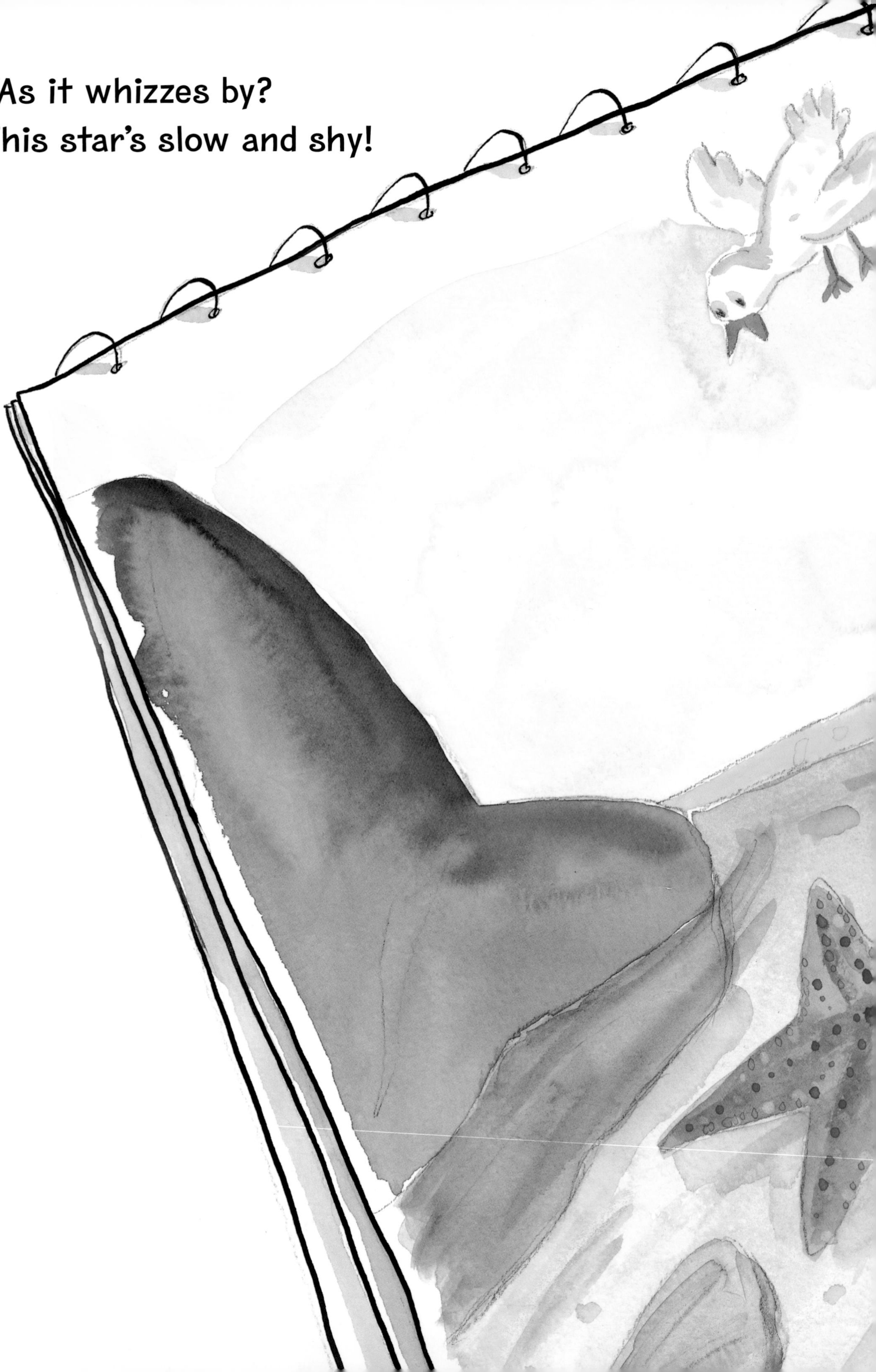

It gracefully glides
On tiny tube feet,
Searching the tide pools
For a mollusk to eat."

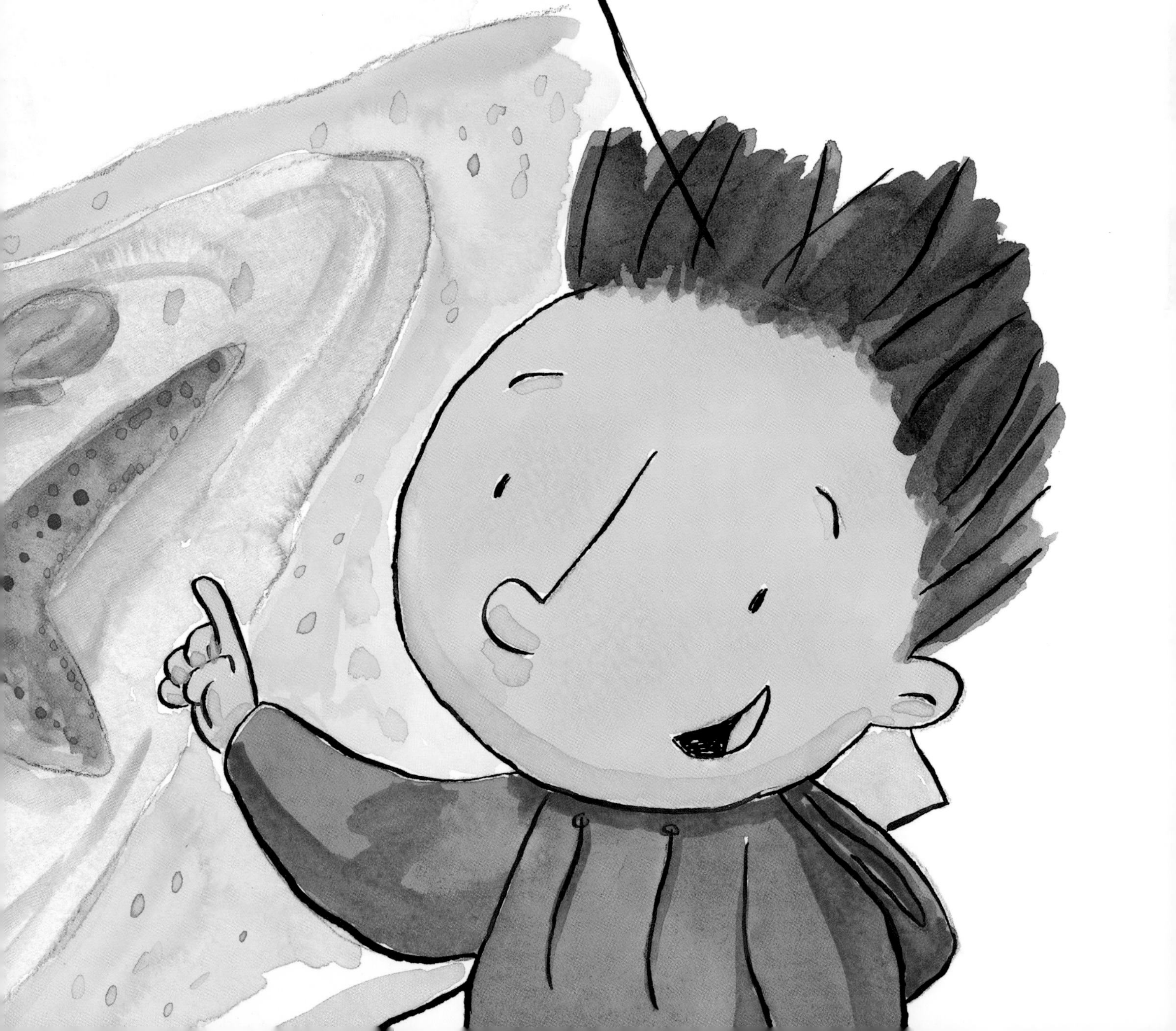

"It's clear to me, Jack!
And thank you, my friend—
I'm so sad that my visit
Has come to an end."

"You really must go?
Well, if that is so,
Please come again, Flash,
And I'll show you more
Mysteries and wonders
That we can explore!"